THE STORY of LIGHT

SUSAN L. ROTH

MORROW JUNIOR BOOKS
NEW YORK

Acknowledgments

The Story of Light was inspired by a Cherokee myth. Variations can be found in many anthologies of Native American legends.

I would like to acknowledge these Native American specialists: Victor Golla, Department of Anthropology, Humboldt State University, Arcata, California; Cesare Marino, Smithsonian Institution, Washington, D.C.; Ed and Kay Sharpe of Cherokee Publications, Cherokee, North Carolina.

I would also like to thank my teachers of woodcut printmaking: Robert Dhaemers, Un-ichi Hiratsuka, and Keiko Hiratsuka Moore.

And I would like to thank Frank Kohn and his colleagues at the National Zoo in Washington, D.C.

Library of Congress Cataloging-in-Publication Data
Roth, Susan L.
The story of light / Susan Roth.
p.   cm.
Summary: A Native American folktale which explains how the
animals brought light into their world.
ISBN 0-688-08676-4.—ISBN 0-688-08677-2 (lib. bdg.)
1. Indians of North America—Legends. [1. Indians of North
America—Legends.] I. Title.
E98.F6R73 1990
398.2'08997—dc20
[E]   90-5654
CIP
AC

For
Mercedes
Love,
Susan

It was dark...

before the sun came.
The animal people
couldn't see,
though thcy had
heard the sun was
alive
on the other side of the world.
They met together in darkness,
bumping into each other,
stepping on each other's
animal feet;
and they decided it was
foolish
to keep living in such
darkness
when all they had to do was
take some of the sun
for themselves.

But which one of them would go?
Bear lumbered into the animals' circle.
He was eager to help his friends
and he never thought too long about anything.
"I'll get the sun," said Bear.
"Wait just a minute," said Fox.
"You might need an ounce
of my cunning. I'll go."
But when he jumped up to leave,
two yellow eyes blocked his way on the
pitch black path.
"This job is mine," said Wolf.
All the animals cried, "Never you, Wolf!"
Wolf was a wanderer. Once
Wolf got the sun, who knew if he'd
ever return?

Then Possum loomed thick in the middle of the crowd.
"I'll snatch a speck of the sun," he said.
"I'll hide it
in my great bushy tail."
The animals agreed that Possum should go.

So Possum walked east
to the other side of the world,
squinting with pain,
squeezing his eyes shut as the brightness
burned
and burned
even when his eyes were tightly closed.

He shielded his scorched eyes with his sweating paw.
And still feeling fire
and fear,
he came to the sun's spot.
His parched mouth said
O.

Possum stole a spark
of white-hot sun
and stuck it under his beautiful tail.
It singed his fur as he scurried
home to the animal people.
But when he returned,
the spark had gone out
and all that remained
was his charred
black snake of a
tail, and . . .

it was still dark.

Buzzard thought
he knew better.
"I'll keep that sun
far away from my sleek tail feathers," he said.
He smiled a little,
secretly musing on
how much cleverer than
Possum he would be.
"I'll bring sunlight
home
high on the top of
my feathery head."

And he left,
flying east
to the other side of the world.

He soon
snatched a bit of the sun
in his
big strong claws and
he placed it
on top
of his feathery head.

But the spark set a
feather on fire,
then another
then another,
and by the time he got home
there were no feathers
left on the top of
his head, only ash;
the spark had burnt out, and . . .

it was still dark.

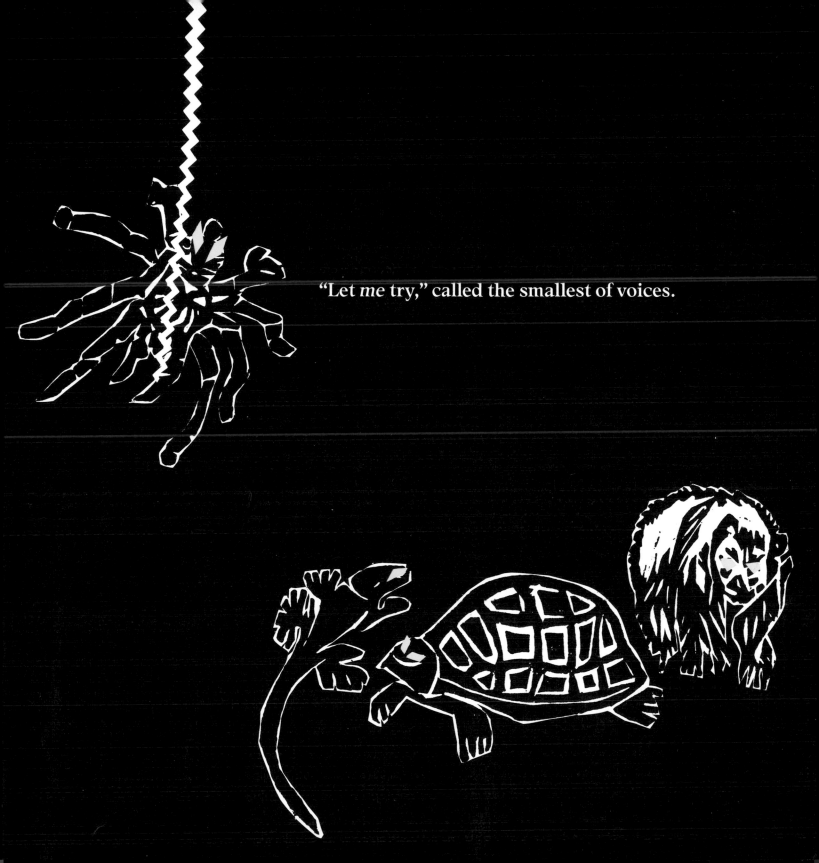

"Let *me* try," called the smallest of voices.

"Let *me* try," the voice insisted. It was only Spider, swinging above all the animal people.

"You? You're too small," said the bears.
"And too old," said the foxes.
"You're a woman," said the wolves.

"Never mind that," called out Spider.
She swung down
to the earth,
took damp clay, and
with her tiny hands
she molded
a pot.

Then she walked
to the east, spinning
her thread,
and she followed
the rays of the sun
as they bent to lead her through
the shadowy grass.

Spider's pot first turned leather-hard
in the cool dark of her slow walk.
And as the day grew
lighter and hotter, so the pot grew
harder and drier.

It was a long walk
for Spider.
At the sun's spot
she took the smallest of sparks
to hide in her little clay pot. She
turned around slowly
and followed her thread
back to the west,
lighting her way
with the sun
in her pot.

And this was how
Spider
brought the sun to her
animal people. It's The
Story of Light....

And even today
Possum shuns the sun;
he still has a tail with
no fur; and
Buzzard still has a head with
no feathers; and
Spider's webs still
look like sun's rays; and
pots are still dried
slowly in the shadows
before they are baked
in a very hot oven.

The end.